Giuseppe M. A. Baretti, Samuel Sharp, William Nicoll

A View of the Customs, Manners, Drama &c. of Italy

as they are described in the Frusta letteraria, and in The account of Italy in

English, written by Mr. Baretti, compared with The letters from Italy,

written by Mr. Sharp

Giuseppe M. A. Baretti, Samuel Sharp, William Nicoll

A View of the Customs, Manners, Drama &c. of Italy
*as they are described in the Frusta letteraria, and in The account of Italy in English,
written by Mr. Baretti, compared with The letters from Italy, written by Mr. Sharp*

ISBN/EAN: 9783337239114

Printed in Europe, USA, Canada, Australia, Japan

Cover: Foto ©Andreas Hilbeck / pixelio.de

More available books at **www.hansebooks.com**

A

V I E W

OF THE

CUSTOMS, MANNERS, DRAMA, &c.

OF

I T A L Y,

AS THEY ARE DESCRIBED IN

THE FRUSTA LETTERARIA;

AND IN

The Account of ITALY in Englifh,

Written by Mr. B A R E T T I ;

COMPARED WITH

The L E T T E R S from I T A L Y,

Written by Mr. S H A R P.

By SAMUEL SHARP, Efq;

LONDON:

Printed for W. Nicoll, No. 51, in St. Paul's Church-Yard,

M DCC LXVIII.

[Price One Shilling and Six-pence.]

ADVERTISEMENT.

MR. Sharp had nearly finifhed this Pamphlet, before he intended to prefix his Name to it, which may ferve as an Apology, if an Apology be neceffary, for its being written in the third Perfon.

Mr. Sharp has not fcrupled to afcribe the *Frufta Letteraria* to Mr. Baretti, having feen feveral Gentlemen who have heard him fpeak of himfelf as the Author.

A

V I E W

OF THE

CUSTOMS, MANNERS, DRAMA, &c.

OF

I T A L Y.

IN the years 1763, 64, and 65, Mr. Baretti carried on at Venice, an anonymous periodical work, called the *Frusta Letteraria*, (or Literary Scourge) not unlike our Critical Review, in which he has not only passed his judgment on a variety of books published in Italy ; but also from time to time has occasionally given us a picture of the manners of Italy in that period. As Mr. Baretti is an Italian by birth, and lived at that juncture, in the midst of his countrymen, we must suppose him labouring under all the honest prejudices, in favour of his native country, to which the wisest men are subject ; so that possibly some allowance should be made for the flattery of his pencil ; but of this the reader will judge by and by.

B

Mr.

Mr. Baretti in the Englifh account has thrown out feveral animadverfions on Mr. Sharp's Letters from Italy; and indeed they feem to have given birth to that work. My principal defign therefore in this pamphlet, is to examine the opinions advanced in thofe letters, of which the *Frufta Letteraria* will be no improper criterion, as it will be imagined that Mr. Baretti, when he gave the publick his thoughts on the Learning, Drama, Poetry, and Manners of his native country, fpoke the dictates of his heart, and to the beft of his judgment, the truth, without fallacy or difguife.

I do not think it a matter of any confequence, whether Mr. Sharp was dreaming, drunk, or mad, when he wrote thofe Letters, or even whether it was not he himfelf, but his footman, who was the author of them; all which facts are afferted by Mr. Baretti. My inquiry fhall be into the truth of the relations, which are publifhed under the name of Mr. Sharp, and I fhall be cautious in calling upon any other authority, than the writings of Mr. Baretti himfelf.

The charge of omiffion is very fevere againft Mr. Sharp. He is upbraided with fome bitternefs,

nefs, for having wilfully neglected to fpeak of the literature of Italy, from an averfion to do juftice and honour to its learned men. I will not take upon me to be refponfible for Mr. Sharp's filence on that head ; perhaps he did not prefume to touch upon fo delicate a fubject, being confcious that to be mafter of it requires both time and fcience ; perhaps he had formed a difadvantageous judgement of the prefent ftate of learning in Italy, and was too diffident of his abilities, to publifh that judgement ; or, laftly, perhaps, he had conceived a favourable opinion of it, but meeting with Mr. Baretti's *Frufta Letteraria*, where the feveral articles of literature are fo differently treated, he might drop his pen, and fubmit his ideas, to thofe of fo good a critic as Mr. Baretti.——To give therefore a farther infight into the prefent ftate of literature in Italy, than what is to be obtained from any other writings, I fhall in the courfe of this paper, offer Mr. Baretti's thoughts on this fubject, as they appear in his *Frufta Letteraria*; but firft, I fhall extract from his Englifh account, in as concife a manner as I am able, his prefent opinion on this article.

In his 13th chapter he afks, " to what end did Mr. Sharp give an account of his travels

through

through Italy, if he did not visit our several universities, and enter our numerous libraries? What judgement would posterity form of Italy from an account given by him, who had no personal acquaintance with any one of the many men of learning that live at present amongst us?" In other parts of this chapter, he compares the present age with the illustrious age of Leo 10th; and says, that when he considers the wonderful progress, that all sciences have made all over Europe, within these three last centuries, he is almost tempted to think, that exclusive of the knowledge of learned languages, the real knowledge of the present English women alone, were it possible to bring it all together, would prove not much inferior to the real knowledge of that illustrious age, with which shallow satirists, and peevish poets, of all countries, reproach the degeneracy of their own.——After this panegyrick on the English ladies, which possibly may offend the Italian ladies as a satire on them, Mr. Baretti proceeds to give us a long catalogue of libraries and learned men now in Italy, and affirms that in all their universities every kind of literature is much cultivated, and that every one of them can boast of some eminent professor.　　　　　　　　　　　　In

In chapter the 14th, he treats at length on the education of phyficians and furgeons, with great encomiums on their practice, which he extends even to the practitioners of fmall towns and villages. In this chapter he alfo defcribes the manner in which ftudents in divinity and ftudents in law, are qualified for the church and the bar; and here he takes occafion to join with Mr. Sharp in condemning the noify method of pleading at Venice:—His words are;—Mr. Sharp in the very beginning of his work, fets out, foppifhly enough, for a deep critick in the Venetian dialect, and fpeaks of the advocates of Venice; yet he does not venture to give his opinion with regard to their powers in oratory. He only defcribes them in their acts of peroration, and is very right when he fays, that their voices are difcord, their gefticulations approaching to thofe of madmen, and their general way of pleading, noify and uncivilized."——I cannot difmifs this paragraph, without obferving, how unkindly Mr. Baretti has perverted the fenfe of Mr. Sharp's remark on the inability of many Venetians, to pronounce the letter G, &c. reprefenting him as having coined the Venetian words, Dudice, Dulio, &c; whereas Mr.

Sharp

Sharp only afferts, that through this inability, the Venetians pronounce the words Giudice, Giulio, &c. as if they were written Dudice, Dulio, &c. (p. 5.) I beg pardon for this digreffion ; but to render the comparative view of thefe two writers clear and diftinct, it may be neceffary, now and then, to adjuft a mifreprefentation, when it occurs ; that we may form a true judgment of their different opinions.

Mr. Baretti, in his eulogium on the learned men of Italy, laments however, the difcouragements under which learning lies, and afcribes its prefent vigour, to the ambition and curiofity of its admirers. He fays, that learning cannot procure in our days, that veneration to its poffeffors from all claffes of people, and efpecially from princes and great lords, which it procured to them foon after its reftoration ; that a cardinal's hat is not now to be grafped at by climbing up the ladders of Greek and Latin ; that they have no King of Pruffia for a patron and panegyrift, who will deign to take the trouble of gilding all Voltaire's filver, and all Algarotti's copper ; that the trade of writing books is by no means a profitable trade ; that not one writer in a hundred, ever got with his quill as much in a twelvemonth, as the worft hackney fcribler

fcribler in London can get in a week; that the impoffibility of making money by their literary labours, is not the only difadvantage that attends the learned of Italy; they are likewife to encounter many difficulties in the publication of their works. Nothing is printed in Italy without being firft licenfed by two, and fometimes more revifers, appointed by the civil and ecclefiaftical government. Thefe are to perufe every manufcript intended for the prefs; and fometimes their fcrupuloufnefs and timidity, fometimes their vanity or ill temper, and fometimes their ignorance and infufficiency, raife fo many objections, that a poor author is often made quite fick with his own productions. Yet he fays, that long ufe has reconciled the Italians to this cuftom; and that in the prefent ftate of things, flavery is preferable to liberty. Had Mr. Sharp drawn the Italians in the black colours here exhibited by Mr. Baretti, he might reafonably have incurred the indignation, not only of Italians, but of every man who has any fenfe of the bleffings of liberty. Were our prefs to be fet free, fays Mr. Baretti, fedition, defamation, profanenefs, ribaldry, and other fuch benefits, would then quickly circulate through all our towns, villages, and hamlets. Irreli-

gion

gion would be fubftituted in a great meafure to
bigotry and fuperftition ; the Pope would be
called antichrift, and mother church a whore ;
fuch would be, amongft others, the bleffed effect of a free prefs in Italy, could we ever be
indulged with it. But Heaven avert we fhould !
It is faid that no body knows the pleafures of
madnefs but madmen. The fame may be
juftly faid of the peculiar advantages of flavery ;
they are not to be conceived but by flaves.
And if it be true, that learning cannot flourifh,
but in the fun-fhine of liberty ; and if it be
impoffible, without a freedom of the prefs,
ever to have in Italy fuch writers as the John-
fons and Warburtons of England, let Italy
never have any, as long as their Alps and Ap-
penines will ftand ; provided that on the other
hand fhe never be ornamented by — Cætera
defunt.

I fhall not defcant on this account of the
general ftate of learning in Italy, which feems
on the one hand, to be reprefented as in the
moft flourifhing fituation ; and on the other,
as labouring under almoft infurmountable difficulties ; but fhall proceed to the pofitive judgement that Mr. Baretti has paffed on this fubject in his *Frufta Letteraria*,

Frusta Letteraria.

Page 290. Mr. Baretti afferts, that in point of learning the Italians are as far below the French, as the people of Morocco are below the Italians.

P. 191. That amongft the modern Tufcans, Cocchi alone writes a perfectly good profe—all the others, are totally ignorant of a good ftile. Count Gafparo Gozzi of Venice, however, approaches towards his manner, as does alfo a young profeffor at Padua, whofe name I do not mention, becaufe he has never printed any book.—All the Romans and Neapolitans write badly; I mean with regard to ftile.— In Piedmont and in Lombardy, I do not know any author who writes diftinguifhably well.— This account perhaps (fays Mr. Baretti) does no great honour to my dear country; but fhall I tell lies to do honour to my dear country?

P. 329. He affirms that 'till within thefe two or three years, for half a century paft, fonnets, eclogues, love ftanzas, &c. have infected all Italy; and that this poetical peftilence has, during that period, committed the moft cruel

devaf-

devaftation on logic, good tafte and common fenfe.

P. 381. That amongft the innumerable falfe opinions which are adopted in wife Italy, for true ones, that which Italians form in regard to their language, is not the leaft falfe; as they fuppofe without fcruple, that it is fuperior, in beauty, to all the living languages; and that it even equals thofe of Greece and ancient Rome; but that he fhall fhew them, with clear evidence, the falfity of this notion, and prove to them, that their language is not equal, much lefs fuperior, to the living languages of France and England.

P. 168. That in Italy there are, at this time, more writers than readers; but that there are only three authors generally read; one a good writer, Meteftafio; the other two, Goldoni and Chiari, bad writers.

P. 253. That however Italy may not be fo totally deftitute of accomplifhed ladies, as fome women-haters would make us believe; neverthelefs we muft, to our fhame, confefs, that our ladies are not generally educated with the fame attention, as in other parts of Europe. In France, Germany, and even in Denmark and

and Sweden, it is as eafy to find many women perfectly well educated, and confequently knowing and amiable, as in this our peninfula, to meet with foolifh and ill behaved women ; neverthelefs the blame of this difgraceful difference betwixt *all* our ladies, and *all* the ladies of thofe countries, is not to be imputed entirely to our fathers and mothers, though they fcandaloufly neglect this their principal duty, but in great part to the writers in Italy, who have not yet been able to fupply their country with proper books for finifhing a woman's education.

P. 311. Mr. Baretti treating of *L' Offervatore Veneto*, written in imitation of the Englifh Spectators, by the Count Gafparo Gozzi, fpeaks highly of that performance, and fays, that would every body, men and women, read Gozzi, in Italy, as all ranks of people have read the Spectators in England, he fhould expect the fame benefits from it ; but that he cannot flatter himfelf with the hopes of feeing his dear countrymen do fo good a thing ; becaufe that his dear countrymen univerfally do not love to read books which are calculated to improve them.

P. 9.

P. 9. Speaking favourably of a book entitled, *Della Prefervatione della falute de Letterati*, he fays, that in certain countries, every woman juft above the vulgar would have read it ; but that in Italy, he would bet one of his teeth, that no woman has opened it. It is enough in Italy, that a book have a learned title, to prevent it from being univerfally read ; whereas on the contrary, in England, and in Holland, ay in frozen Denmark and Sweden, nay in the frightful country of Norway, and even in horrible Finland, the habitation of the cold North wind————

Vol. 2. p. 7. He fays, that on the firft appearance of the *Frufta Letteraria*, it was judged a ufeful and neceffary work, in a country like theirs, over-run on every fide with foolifh literature and indecent manners.——

Vol. 1. p. 11. Mr. Baretti, cenfuring two certain publications, fays however, that thanks to the great ignorance of the great number of his countrymen, they were univerfally read for fome time.

P. 237. Do not call upon me to prove that dullnefs is the principal and univerfal characteriftick of our modern writers, fince it is a fact fo apparent, and confequently fo eafy to prove, that

that I know nothing more eafy of demonftration.

P. 393. Amongft other languages which Mr. Baretti recommends to the ftudy of the Italians, he particularly fpecifies Englifh, in which many, very many excellent books are written, that they have never heard of; would they tranflate fome of thefe into Italian, they would, fays he, extend the limits of their prefent knowledge, and they would act much more laudably, than to be for ever flattering this or that great Lord, in hopes of a dinner or a few ducats.

P. 316. Mr. Baretti affirms, that the practice of furgery, all over Italy, abounds with a multiplicity of remedies; is filthy, ftinking, and pompous; becaufe the practitioners are ignorant of what is fimple and true; and that the phyficians of Italy would fpare many lives, or as he expreffes it, commit fewer homicides, if they would render their practice more fimple.

A Soliloquy of Mr. Baretti.

P. 317. What! faid I often to myfelf, is this noble country then a privy, where every dirty fellow has a right to drop the excrements

of

of his brain? Is it poffible that no means fhould
have been found, to prevent this naftinefs in
our literature; or at leaft, to cure fome of
thefe bare breeched rafcals of their diarrhæa?

Vol. 2. p. 57. In a chapter to which he has
given the title of *the glories of the age of dark-*
nefs, he fays, If in future times, any learned
men fhall compile the infipid literary hiftory
of modern Italy, I beg my name may not be
mentioned amongft thofe of my countrymen;
and my ghoft will be much obliged to them,
if they will inform their cotemporaries, that I
never fpoke of the age I lived in, but under the
title of Tenebrofo; and a few lines lower, he
calls it an age, with refpect to Italy, dark, very
dark—Tenebrofo, Tenebrofiffimo.——I fhall
make no comment on thefe bold ftrokes, and
feeming caricatures; but the reader, I fuppofe,
will, after this reprefentation, forbear to cenfure Mr. Sharp's total filence on the ftate of
learning in Italy; as it is natural to believe,
that however wide his opinions may have been
from thofe advanced in the *Frufta Letteraria,*
by Mr. Baretti, yet he could hardly dare to
oppofe the judgment of a man, who was a critick by profeffion, and who being an Italian,

was

was fo much better qualified than he could be, to write on fo difficult a fubject.

Mr. Baretti, in the 15th chapter of the Englifh account, finifhes the article of literature, with a defcription of the feveral academies now fubfifting, or that have fubfifted in Italy. The academy of the Crufca, ftands the foremoft in rank, and was inftituted at Florence in the 16th century, for the purpofe of afcertaining the Italian language, which undertaking it accomplifhed, with great honour to the members: at prefent it is declining, becaufe all that could be faid upon the fubject, has been faid over and over.

Next to the academy Della Crufca, that of the Arcadia Romana rofe in repute. The bufinefs of the Arcadia Romana was to correct, increafe, and beautify our poetry; as that of the Crufca, to purify, illuftrate and fix our language. The members of this fociety, affumed the characters of fhepherds, and it is one of the fundamental laws, that no perfon fhall be admitted a member, without firft taking upon him a paftoral name.—The fame of this academy foon fpread all over Italy, and fiftyeight towns refolved on a fudden, to have like academies of their own, which they unanimoufly

moufly called colonies of the Roman Arcadia.
Mr. Baretti, however, concludes this account
with informing us, that the Arcadian colonies
are at laft nearly annihilated throughout Italy ;
and the Arcadia Romana confifts now only of a
few Abatinos; but they ftill chufe a chief
herdfman, whofe moft important bufinefs, is
to make a penny of his place, and this he
chiefly effects by fending Arcadian patents to
the Englifh travellers on their arrival at
Rome.

I fhall now give the reader an extract from
the *Frufta Letteraria*, on thefe two academies; and I am much miftaken, if he will
not find both profit and pleafure, from what
Mr. Baretti has advanced in his ftrictures on the
dictionary of the Crufca.

FRUSTA LETTERARIA.

P. 381. Though the Vocabulary of the
Crufca, contain four thoufand more words,
than either Johnfon's Dictionary, or that of
the French Academy; yet one third of them
are not ufed, either in writing, or in converfation ; whereas both the Englifh, and French,
adopt in a manner every word in their dictionaries.

tionaries. Mr. Baretti thinks it would be of utili-
ty to the publick, were the vocabulary purged
of the various kinds of obfolete, and certain
obfcene words with which it abounds. He
laments that the antient and prefent members of
the academy, being moftly Florentines, have
always prefcribed to authors, the ufe of the
Tufcan language. He fays that in France, the
language of books is the fame through the
whole kingdom ; and that in England, the
fame rule is obferved ; but that in Italy, authors
are conftrained to ftudy the dialect of a particular country, which would not have been the
cafe, had the vocabulary of the Crufca, been
a univerfal, and not a provincial vocabulary.
Another objection to their vocabulary, is their
choice of words from infamous and vulgar
writers ; whereas in England, the models of
the language are the writings of Clarendon,
Temple, Swift, &c. and in France, the Corneilles, the Racines, the Molieres, are their
models, all venerable names ;—and, fays he,
fhall we Italians number amongft the authors
of our language, a croud of fcriveners, barbers,
coopers, carpenters, and fuch like rabble ?
Can a language written in the times of barba-
rifm, when we knew neither fcience nor criti-

C   cifm,

cifm, ftand in any competition with the languages written by Boffuet and Tillotfon?
What ample dictionaries would thofe of England and France be, if the French ftill regif-
tered the words ufed by Amift, Rabelais, Co-
mines ; and the Englifh preferved thofe of
Gower, Chaucer and Caxton? He finifhes
this critique on the Italian vocabulary, with an
obfervation on Boccace, which as I efteem it
equally curious with all the opinions advanced
under this article, I fhall beg leave to lay before the reader.——

" Boccace had wit, a lively imagination,
eloquence, and all the other endowments neceffary to form a good writer ; neverthelefs
Boccace has been the ruin of the Italian tongue,
and the chief caufe that Italy does not yet pof-
fefs a good and univerfal language; becaufe
thefe writers who firft fucceeded him, and afterwards the academifts of the Crufca, delighted with his writings, the beft they had yet
feen, and charmed more than they fhould have
been with the wantonnefs of his pen, they
went on from year to year, and from age to
age, celebrating him fo much, that at length the
univerfal opinion, or rather the univerfal error,
was eftablifhed; that in point of language and
ftyle,

ftyle, Boccace was abfolutely without a fault ; and confequently that whoever would write well in Italian, ought to write as Boccace had written.—But how can it be believed, that a man who lived in an age nearly barbarous, could perfect the language of our country ? that a fervile imitator of the tranfpofed phrafes of the Latin, a dead language, could be the original of his own, a living one ? Neverthelefs fuch was the refpect paid to his works, that for the fpace of two hundred years, hardly any writer prefumed to adopt a word not confecrated in them. This is the reafon why our written language ftill retains the Latin character, and that people in general cannot be pleafed with the writings of Boccace, nor his followers : whilft in England and in France, where they fortunately had no Boccace, nor difciples of Boccace, there have been formed two written languages, equally intelligible to the higheft and the loweft orders of men."

ARCADIA ROMANA.

Page 1ſt. Mr. Baretti opens his account of a book entitled Hiſtorical Memoirs of the aſſembly of the Arcadians, in the following manner :

Thoſe admirers of unprofitable knowledge, who not being able to ſpend their time to advantage, employ it in learning trifles, and are deſirous of being informed of that moſt celebrated literary puerility, called Arcadia, let them read this book. The author has written it with that feeblenefs of ſtile, and that humble ſpirit of adulation, which principally cha
racteriſes the Arcadians. In the firſt chapter we have the names of the firſt fourteen founders of the Arcadian inſtitution, eleven of which, ſays Mr. Baretti, are buried in oblivion, and the remaining three, Gravina, Creſcembini, and Zappi, have their defects. Gravina underſtood Latin and juris-prudence ; but unhappily, in ſpite of Nature, he would be a poet, when ſhe meant him to be an advocate. Creſcembini was a man whoſe fancy was compounded partly of wood, and partly of lead ; but he foretells that Zappi, the amorous, the gallant, the

the fugary Zappi, will continue to be read by
all young noble ladies, a month before, and a
month after marriage, and that he will float on
the furface of Lethe, without finking, fo long
as the tafte of effeminate (Eunuca) poetry fhall
fubfift in Italy.

The fecond chapter, he fays, tires us with
the laws of Arcadia, which are written in imitation of thofe of antient Rome ; but are as
unlike them, as an ape is to a doctor of the
Sorbonne, or (as he expreffes it in page 54 of
the 2d vol.) as the ftatue of Harlequin, to the
real perfon of Julius Cæfar.

The utter contempt with which he treats
this fociety in his remarks on the two firft
chapters, renders it needlefs to give any farther proofs of the low eftimation in which he
holds it.

Mr. Baretti, in the 15th chapter of the Englifh account, fays, that befides the poor remains
of the Crufca and the Arcadia, there are in Rome,
and in other towns, other academies compofed
of people who pretend to ingenuity in one thing
or other. At Rome, the academy of St. Luke
have chofen St. Luke for their patron ; and he
tells us, that the fearchers into antient records,
pretend, that in the 12th century there lived

one

one Maſtro Luca, whoſe chriſtian name was
Santo, and that this man carved the famous
Madonas of Loretto, Bologna, &c. whence
aroſe the vulgar notion that thoſe Madonas
were painted by St. Luke : However, Mr.
Baretti ſpeaks with ſome diffidence of this ſcrap
of erudition, and admits that the famous *Neu-
ſtra Sennora del Pillar* actually worſhipped in
Saragozza, and that ſtill more famous Madona
of Monſerrate in Catalonia, were really, in the
opinion of the Spaniards, the works of St.
Luke. He might have added, that the Madona of Bologna, is really believed at Bologna,
to have been painted by St. Luke, and thus
have ſpared himſelf the trouble of begging Mr.
Sharp's pardon, for his ridiculous digreſſion
(as he calls it) in honour of their Madonas ;
ſince Mr. Sharp has only ſaid the very ſame
thing, namely, that many Madonas in Europe
are ſuppoſed to have been painted by St. Luke.

At Florence, about Galileo's time, was in-
ſtituted the *Accademia del Cimento,* or of ex-
perimental philoſophy. It did not laſt long ;
but it is now ſucceeded by the *Accademia
d'Agricoltura,* and if Mr. Baretti is not miſtaken, by La Societa Columbaria, whoſe members apply to natural philoſophy, and moſt
particularly

particularly to botany. There are befides in other towns, other academies ; and he quotes Francefco Saverio Quadrio, who has written on this fubject, and who affirms that there are above five hundred academies in Italy.—I fhall finifh this article with the conclufion of the 15th chapter, which poffibly may appear to be a moft remarkable anticlimax fo foon after the pompous mention of five hundred academies. I own, fays Mr. Baretti, that arts and fciences are not generally forwarded much by our academies, as far as I can obferve ; yet they are upon the whole, rather ufeful than pernicious, and anfwer the ends of fociety, if not of fcience ; they ftand in the place of the clubs in England, which bring people together, and give them the means of becoming friends.

Englifh

Englifh Account of the Italian Drama.

12th and 13th Chap.—Mr. Sharp is guilty
of the moft ridiculous felf-conceit, when he
fpeaks at large of the prefent ftate of the Italian ftage; let any man unacquainted with Italy
read his five letters on the Italian ftage, and
he will prefently conclude, that the Italians
are a people moft miferably ignorant of theatri-
cal matters ; that they have banifhed all fenfe
and propriety from their dramas, and that they
cannot be pleafed with any thing but farcical
buffoonery.—But is this giving a true idea of
their ftage ?—Certainly not—The mighty
cenfurer ought, &c.—Let us therefore collect
what Mr. Sharp has advanced on this fubject,
and compare it with the information which
Mr. Baretti has given us himfelf.

Letter 23. Mr. Sharp tells us, that the play-
houfe at Naples labours under great difcouragements ; that only the lower fort of people frequent it ; that the price of the pit is four-pence
half-penny, and that it does not hold above
eighty people ; that he never faw a tragedy
there ; and that all the comedies he had been
at, confifted of three acts only ; that Punch,

the

the Doctor's Man, &c. were the characters, who, with their obscenities and extempore wit, in the Neapolitan dialect, delighted the populace; but that in his opinion, the Italians by nature have a genius for comedy; and were the audience more elegant, and more respectable, their actors would appear to have great talents.

Letters 47 and 48. At Florence, Mr. Sharp says, their theatre is much superior to that of Naples, but speaks of their comedies as he does afterwards of those at Turin, (Letter 51) as affording diversion, from mistaking one word for another, blunders, indelicate jokes, &c. and as the price of the pit is only six-pence, he does not see any prospect of the Italian stage being raised to the dignity which it might obtain, were poets and players honoured, protected and rewarded by their princes. He saw for the first time there a comedy of five acts, and a tragedy translated from Voltaire, upon which occasion he speaks very favourably of the declamation of the stage; and I believe this is the substance of what he has said upon the tragedy and comedy of Italy.

Mr. Baretti, in the 12th chapter of his English account, asserts, that as soon as the names

of Corneille and Racine began to be commonly
known in Italy, many good tragedies were
written upon the French model by the wits of
thofe times; and of late, almoft all the tragedies of Corneille, Racine, Crebillon, and Voltaire, have been tranflated into blank verfe,
and reprefented. But, he fays, the polite people cannot fill a play-houfe, and the vulgar
cannot as yet be brought to relifh fuch compofitions, and they would ftill have kept invaria-
bly faithful to their Harlequins, Pantaloons,
Brighellas, and the other mafks, if Goldoni
and Chiari, two dramatick writers, had not fud-
denly made their appearance about eighteen or
twenty years ago. Both thefe writers are
equally contemptible in the eyes of Mr. Baretti; but he fpeaks highly of the talents of
Carlo Gozzi, younger brother to Count Gafparo Gozzi, who has brought ten or twelve plays
on the ftage, two or three of which Mr. Baretti has perufed in manufcript; but he fays,
the author cannot be prevailed on to publifh
them. However he arraigns Mr. Sharp in
the conclufion of this letter, for not having
mentioned Carlo Gozzi and Metaftafio; for-
getting that Metaftafio's works are compofitions
for the opera-houfe, and not within the defcription

ſcription undertaken by Mr. Sharp: And as to Carlo Gozzi, if Mr. Sharp had never the honour to peruſe his manuſcripts, and was ſo unfortunate to be at Venice when the theatres were ſhut, as he tells us in letter 4th, with what propriety could he have ſpoken of that excellent writer? But Mr. Sharp might here with great propriety aſk Mr. Baretti why he has not mentioned the name of Carlo Gozzi in his *Fruſta Letteraria.*

I ſhall now bring forth Mr. Baretti's ſentiments on this ſubject, extracted from his *Fruſta Letteraria,* by which it will appear that his judgment of the Italian ſtage, is exactly, or nearly the ſame, with that of Mr. Sharp, though perhaps, expreſſed a little more harſhly ; but firſt I ſhall borrow his thoughts on the Italian ſtage, as he has given them in his Italian Library, publiſhed at London 1757.

Page 124. At preſent we have nothing in Italy but muſical operas, like thoſe exhibited at the Opera-houſe in the Haymarket, and a kind of plays commonly divided into three acts, and recited extempore, by different companies of low-witted fellows. The ſerious parts, as they call them, are in Tuſcan, (not of the beſt indeed): The comical parts by Pantalone,

Arlecchino,

Arlecchino, Brighella, Dottore, Coviello; and some others speaking various dialects of Italy.— If they make people laugh with their repartees, and immoral jests, they have an audience; if not, they stare. Our old and good tragedies and comedies, are confined to colleges, and seminaries, where students act them in the carnival time.

One would gather from the above recited paragraph, that the Italians, in the year 1757, represented no other species of comedy, than the extempore comedy; and from the paragraph a little before it, relating to Goldoni and Chiari, that upon the appearance of those writers about 18 or 20 years ago, the Harlequins, Pantaloons, &c. with their extempore wit, had been driven off the stage; but neither of these facts are strictly true, as I shall evince from some of Goldoni's prefaces.

Goldoni tells us, that till the year 1742, he did not write any comedy, where he had composed all the parts; for, before that period, he had written only one or two of the principal characters, and the outlines of the rest, leaving it to the extempore wit of the actors to fill up the parts; that before his time, for above a century past, the comic stage had

been

been in fo corrupt a ftate, and the humour of
it fo wretchedly low and vulgar, that it excited
the laughter of the mob only ; and had brought
contempt upon it from all the neighbouring king-
doms. Urged therefore by the defire of glory, he had attempted a reformation, and had
now written the parts for the mafked characters, having found from experience, that when
they were left open to the extempore wit of the
players, provided they could make their audience laugh, they generally faid what came
uppermoft, without any regard to the fcope
of the play, and the character of the part they
reprefented.

It appears therefore from Goldoni, that the
Harlequins, the Pantaloons, &c. remain on the
Italian ftage to this day; with the difference
only, that many of their parts are written for
them ; but look into his plays, and you will
find the fame humour, and the fame characters,
fpeaking the different dialects of Naples, Bologna, Venice, &c. (fo indifpenfable to an
Italian audience) as it was the cuftom to exhi-
bit in the days of their extempore comedy.

Neverthelefs I would not have it under-
ftood, that the players are entirely reftrained
from extempore wit at this juncture : it abounds

upon

upon the Neapolitan ftage, and fpreads itfelf more or lefs, through all the theatres of Italy, to the Italian comedy at Paris; where Carlin the Harlequin entertains the Parifians with an inexhauftible fund of this fpecies of humour.

As Goldoni is much fpoken of; and has furnifhed the Italian ftage with a prodigious number of comedies; it may poffibly be acceptable to an Englifh reader to hear a few anecdotes of him. Goldoni was defigned for the bar; but his genius leading him to the cultivation of the drama, he affociated himfelf with a company of comedians, travelling from city to city; and fupplying them with new comedies, whenever they ftood in need of them: He tells us that he undertook to furnifh fixteen comedies in one year, befides fmall pieces which were fet to mufick.—If Goldoni therefore, be ever fo diftant from Moliere, (a name his favourers have honoured him with) the difadvantage he lay under, from writing fo rapidly, and writing for an audience fo unpolifhed, is fome excufe for his defects. Voltaire has however born fome teftimony to his merit; fpeaks of him as having refcued his country from the tyranny of Harlequin; and applauds the ftile of his wri-

2   tings,

tings, fo far as to have put them into the hands
of the great grandaughter of Corneille, that fhe
may learn from them the Italian language:
which fingle circumftance (fays Mr. Baretti in
his *Frufta Letteraria,* p. 121.) proves that
Voltaire knows juft as much Italian, as he does
Japonefe. Indeed this encomium on Goldoni,
who is very low in the eftimation of Mr. Baretti, has produced very fevere ftrictures on Voltaire; for a few lines farther, fpeaking of his
pretenfions to the knowledge of Spanifh and
Portuguefe, he tells us that Voltaire under-
ftands thofe languages, no better than the Ele-
phants of the Grand Mogul do.—After this
fhort digreffion, let us fee what judgment Mr.
Baretti has paffed on the ftage, in his *Frufta
Letteraria.*

P. 255. Mr. Baretti affirms that all the antient Italian tragedies are of little worth, however pedants may praife them; and that the
antient comedies are fo filly, obfcene and nafty,
that you would be fick in reading of them.

P. 342. He remarks upon Voltaire's unpo-
litenefs in afferting, that Italy is a country fold
to Harlequins, and in poffeffion of Goths; but
checks himfelf upon reflection, and feems to
fubfcribe heartily to the opinion, calling it far-
caftically,

caſtically, a country, where Goldoni and Chiari have found four millions of admirers.——
Goldoni, ſays he, writes a corrupt Italian, com-
poſed of three different languages, of Venice,
Lombardy, and the Romagnnolo.

P. 343. The comedies of Goldoni ſwarm
with groſs errors in language, and in grammar,
with low and vulgar phraſes, and what is
worſe, with ridiculous manners, and maxims
of obſcenity and ribaldry.

P. 344. Mr. Baretti ſays, Should any aſk
me, who is a good dramatick writer, if Goldoni be a bad one? my anſwer is, Gentlemen,
we have neither Corneilles nor Molieres in our
language; therefore we muſt wait till our good
fortune ſends them.

P. 134. He ſays, that Signior Denina (an
author he is ſpeaking of) wonders how it
ſhould happen, that Italy has not one good
writer of tragedy, when her epick poets are ſo
excellent; the reaſon is, ſays Mr. Baretti, that
there are Arioſtos and Taſſos for guides, but
no Corneilles, nor Racines.

I ſhall next enquire into the comparative
view of the cultivation and populouſneſs of
Italy, as it is repreſented by Mr. Baretti; but
in this purſuit, I ſhall examine what Mr. Sharp
has

has really faid, and not what Mr. Baretti makes him fay.—Mr. Sharp, fpeaking of a country in the ecclefiaftical dominions, (vide letter 10) fays, that it affords the moft pleafing images he has feen, of peace and plenty; that the profpect from Mount Vefuvius (letter 40) prefents a view of the moft fertile country in Europe; that he believes the dutchy of Tufcany is ftill better cultivated, than either the dominions of his Holinefs, or of the King of the Two Sicilies; that all Lombardy is fo well cultivated, that he imagines there is not one acre of barren ground, in the whole tract through which he had travelled (letter 49); and in letter 40, he fays, that the foil in the valleys is very rich, and fo exempt from ftones or clay, that he had been many months in Italy before he faw a fpade, &c.—On the other hand, he fpeaks of the defart Campania of Rome, and the barrennefs of certain mountains, betwixt Rome and Naples, which are uncultivated.

With regard to the populoufnefs of Italy, he admits, that though there are not many villages in thofe parts of the dominions of the King of Naples and the Pope, through which he paffed; yet that the towns fwarmed with inhabitants (letter 40:) That in the city of

Naples,

Naples, there are from three to four hundred thoufand inhabitants; and in fo fmall a dutchy as that of Tufcany, he has admitted that the number of inhabitants amounted to near a million.

Neverthelefs Mr. Baretti has, in p. 99, of his Englifh account, charged Mr. Sharp with having exerted his utmoft eloquence, in order to make it believed, that the whole of Italy is uncultivated and unpeopled. Could one have thought it poffible, after this enumeration of facts, that Mr. Baretti fhould have alledged fo ftrange an accufation?

No lefs uncandid is Mr. Baretti in his 4th chapter, where he arraigns Mr. Sharp for having called the Neapolitans, *a nation diabolical in their nature.* Now Mr. Sharp, fo far from impeaching the body of the people collectively, exprefsly harangues, with a kind of gratitude, on the politenefs of the nobility and gentry, and the particular hofpitality with which they treat Englifh travellers (letter 30.) Nor can I find in any part of his book, the leaft imputation on the gentry of Italy; except in what relates to their prefent mode of gallantry. As to the Neapolitan mob, I believe all difinterefted writers have defcribed them as a ferocious

and

and brutal clafs of men; but Mr. Sharp has neverthelefs fpoken of them as more orderly when in good humour, than an Englifh mob, (letter 32,) and diabolical only, when they are exafperated; but alluding to the promptnefs with which their paffions are kindled, he metaphorically, in another letter, fuppofes brimftone in their veins. It can be only to thefe expreffions, that Mr. Baretti muft have referred for the accufation brought againft Mr. Sharp; but furely it will appear a ftrange perverfion of the fenfe, to afcribe that temper to the generality of the kingdom, which he has in that very quotation, with the moft exact precifion, reftrained to the lower people.

Befides, it appears to me, that Mr. Sharp, notwithftanding the allegations of Mr. Baretti to the contrary, takes pleafure in proclaiming the good qualities he found amongft the lower people: he fpeaks of them throughout all Italy, even of the Neapolitan mob, as being totally exempt from the vice of drinking fpirituous liquors; he tells us that the gondaliers at Venice, are a fober body of men, and not dreft in rags like the lower fort of people in England, who fpend all their money in porter, &c; and giving fome account of the poor at Flo-

rence,

rence, (letter 45,) he says, that compare either their habitations, or their children with those of the inhabitants in the skirts of London, and one would blush for the misery and dissolutenefs of our countrymen.

Another charge of the same nature, is that in chapter 29, where Mr. Baretti declares, that from Mr. Sharp's book it appears, that the nobility of Naples have scarcely any sense, wit, virtue or money left. Now it is true, that Mr. Sharp, speaking of their immense estates, denies, excepting in two or three instances, that they are to be compared with those of the English nobility; but he does not say that they have scarcely any money left: and he certainly does no where specify what measure of wit, virtue and sense, is to be found amongst the Neapolitan nobility; or so much as drop a word on the subject: indeed in letter 38, expressing a pardonable warmth for the honour of his native country, he declares it his opinion, that there are in England, more blessings, and more virtues, than are generally met with in other countries: but if Mr. Baretti has applied this paragraph peculiarly to the nobility of Naples, a Frenchman might, with the same propriety, apply it to the court of Versailles, a

Polander

Polander to the Diet at Warfaw, and a Turk to the Divan at Conftantinople.

Mr. Sharp has no where given any particular account of the Italian nobility, excepting in one inftance; where he defcribes the Venetian nobles to be tall; but enters no farther into their character: I fhall, therefore, in aid of this flight fketch, give the reader fome extracts from a defcription at length, of a Venetian noble, from Mr. Baretti's 26th chapter.— " The generality of foreigners fhun the converfation of the Venetian nobles, or grow prefently fick of it, on difcovering that it is too uniform, local, and egotiftical, at the commencement of their acquaintance; but after fome familiarity, one may foon difcover amongft them, fo many inftances of opennefs and referve, of fagacity and imprudence, of courage and timidity, of knowledge and ignorance, and many other oppofite qualities, fo perfectly blended together, in the fame individual, that I know no fet of men in Europe, fo much worth the trouble of being thoroughly fifted, as the noblemen of Venice. With regard to the Venetian people, thofe who want to keep fair with their nobles, or make them friends, have a very ready means of admittance

to

to their kindnefs, by only praifing them in the
fulfomeft terms, making them believe that
their commonwealth is one of the moft formi-
dable powers upon earth, and that themfelves,
individually, are the moft knowing, generous,
and refpectable people in the world : and I do
not know whether it is more fhocking, or
more diverting, to fee how open the generality of the Venetian nobles are to the vileft
flattery."

Mr. Sharp has drawn heavy cenfures upon
him from Mr. Baretti, for the account he has
given us of the frequent murders in Italy; let
us therefore examine what both of them have
advanced upon this fubject. Mr. Sharp afcribes
the frequency of affaffinations to the protection
of the Church; to the difficulty of feizing offenders; to the forms of law, which fuffer
offenders when feized, to efcape; to the few
examples of capital punifhment; and above
all, to the practice of drawing out knives in
their fudden quarrels, and ftabbing inftantly.—
Mr. Sharp afferts, that this is the only kind of
affaffination he heard of, and is known amongft
the lower people only; fo far is he from tax-
ing the whole body of the people, with being
naturally inclined to murder, which Mr. Baretti

upbraids

upbraids him with: nay Mr. Sharp, in ex-
tenuation of the wickedneſs of this practice,
obſerves, that the dreadful effects of theſe
quarrels might be avoided, were the good
Engliſh mode of boxing introduced amongſt
them (letter 38); intimating, that Engliſh-
men muſt give a vent to their paſſions, as well
as Italians ; and had they no other method of
gratifying their revenge but by ſtabbing, murders might be as common in England as in
Italy.

I ſhall now quote two paſſages from Mr.
Baretti's 5th chapter.—In the firſt he ſays,
that the Italians have ſuch quick feelings, that
even a diſreſpectful word, or glance, from an
equal, will ſuddenly kindle a good number of
them, and make them fall on one another
with their knives.——In the ſecond paſſage,
ſpeaking of the difficulty they find in arreſting
an aſſaſſin, he ſays, " then our people, from
a miſtaken principle of humanity, and ſtill
more miſtaken point of honour, will not give
the leaſt aſſiſtance to the officers of juſtice, in
the execution of their duty ; and you might
ſooner bring an Italian to ſuffer martyrdom,
than force him to ſtop any man purſued by
them."

The

The arguments here adduced by Mr. Baretti, give alone a very fatisfactory folution of the queftion, Why are murders fo frequent in Italy? But I fhall, for a farther illuftration of what Mr. Baretti has advanced, lay before the reader an extract from the Abbé Richard, who has fince the date of Mr. Sharp's Letters, publifhed a Defcription of Italy, and whofe accounts are in high efteem. In his 5th vol. p. 237. fpeaking of the frequent affaffinations at Rome, (which however are not fuppofed to be fo numerous as thofe of Naples, which Mr. Sharp treats of) he fays, " The people here are quick and impetuous in their paffions; either oppofition or jealoufy renders them furious: One fees people of the loweft order poignard one another with the moft determined refolution. They have no other way of fighting, to all appearance: They are more afraid of a punch in the ftomach, than a dagger. In this fort of quarrel, they begin with reviling each other in the moft opprobrious manner. When they are provoked to the higheft degree, then he who is in the greateft paffion, draws out his knife, and the other does the fame; which ever of the two ftrikes firft is ufually the conqueror, and if he is not wounded, retires as
tranquilly,

tranquilly, with his nofe in his cloak, as if he had juft withdrawn from an act of devotion. The by-ftanders carry him that is wounded to the hofpital, and all is over ; unlefs by chance, no church is near, and the officers of juftice happen to be upon the fpot to feize him.— Thefe bloody fcenes are very common at Rome ; at leaft there were twenty of them from December 1761, to May, 1762. Paff-ing by the fquare of the rotunda, I faw two peafants quarrelling, and in an inftant one of them was murdered, without caufing any ex-traordinary commotion amongft the numerous populace who were prefent. In the unwhol-fome feafon (Malaria) of July and Auguft, the government takes no notice of thefe affaffina-tions, imputing them to the effects of a violent fermentation in the blood."

I could, if it were neceffary, bring proofs from the mouth of the prefent ingenious and polite cardinal Albani, that executions are rare, and murders numerous, beyond all cre-dibility of proportion ; fo prevalent is the max-im in Italy, that " we have loft already one fubject by murder, therefore we muft not lofe another by execution." But I believe I have faid enough on this interefting fubject, to efta-

blifh

blifh the truth of all that Mr. Sharp has fug-
gefted. Neverthelefs, though the cuftom be
fo different, from the caufes already affigned,
betwixt England and Italy, Mr. Baretti con-
founds the diftinctions, and fays, fuch fhocking accidents will happen amidft the beft and
moft polite nations.

Mr. Baretti will not believe that Mr. Murray, the refident at Venice, told Mr. Sharp
thofe things, which Mr. Sharp declares he did
tell him; nor does he even believe that he
made him frequent vifits. Certainly in this
inftance Mr. Baretti has been ill inftructed;
for I know that Mr. Sharp lived in the greateft
intimacy with Mr. Murray, fo long as five and
thirty years ago; I know likewife, that Mr.
Hamilton himfelf told Mr. Sharp, and feveral
other Englifhmen, the ftory of the five or fix
murderers, who had taken fanctuary in his
palace, and had found means to efcape punifhment; and indeed had not Mr. Hamilton declared the fact publickly, Mr. Sharp would
have been exceedingly culpable to have
made fo free a ufe of the refpectable name
of his Britannick Majefty's minifter.

I have had likewife an opportunity, fince
the publication of Mr. Sharp's letters, to be informed by Sir James Gray himfelf, before he
embarked

embarked for Spain, that the story of the murderer, mentioned by Mr. Sharp, is very true; and that he was so importuned by people of the first rank, to drop the profecution, that he procured the execution of the delinquent, by the single plea, that it was not in his power to comply, without offending the King his mafter. The murderer was executed at Padua, when Sir James was refident at Venice, and not at Naples, as Mr. Baretti by miftake has reprefented it, becaufe Mr. Sharp fpeaks of Sir James Gray, under the name of the late envoy at Naples.

Mr. Baretti is a little difingenuous on the article of fanctuary. He fays, that there are certain parts of Italy, where the church is not a fanctuary for murderers; but that it would be too prolix for him to enter into a detail of the feveral crimes in which the church is, or is not, a fanctuary; and that it is a grofs mifreprefentation in Mr. Sharp, to fay that the church *throughout Italy* fhelters murderers and affaffins. Who would imagine, after fo fingular a defignation, that Mr. Sharp had never expreffed himfelf in thofe words? Yet fo it is, at leaft I cannot difcover them, and Mr. B. for very good reafons, never refers to the

7   page,

page, when he pretends to make a quotation.
If therefore Mr. Sharp has not ufed thofe
words, he muft be fuppofed to have fpoken of
thofe places where he refided, and where he
had an opportunity to be inftructed ; I mean
Naples, Rome, and Florence ; in neither of
which cities, I imagine, Mr. Baretti will deny,
that the church is a fanctuary to affaffins,
though he infinuates as much, when he dif-
putes the reality of an affaffin having taken
fhelter upon the fteps of a certain church near
an Englifh nobleman's palace in Florence, as
related by Mr. Sharp, fufpecting him to be a
pick-pocket, or a fimple robber, and not a murderer, as his lordfhip knew him pofitively to be.

The dirtinefs of the inns on the Loretto
road from Bologna to Rome, and on the road
from Rome to Naples, defcribed in Mr. Sharp's
letters, have mifled many hafty readers of his
letters, to confider them as a fatire on the cuftoms and manners of Italy : and yet even in
this article, where fpeaking the plain truth is
to fpeak fatire, he is fo apprehenfive, that what
he defcribes as peculiar to thofe roads, fhould
be precipitately extended by the reader, to the
accommodation generally found in the inns of
Italy, that he begs his correfpondent to remem-
ber,

ber, that in their great towns, the accommodation is good and cleanly ; in fhort, that the defcription anfwers thofe two roads only, (Letter 45).

But that Mr. Sharp in all probability may have drawn a true picture of thofe inns, may be gathered from the following extract of a letter, dated Naples, October 28, 1766. My correfpondent is a very ingenious gentleman of that city, who fpeaks and writes Englifh, though not in a manner to be compared with Mr. Baretti, whofe proficiency in our language is really a matter of aftonifhment. I fhall give the extract however in his own words, defcribing his journey in company with a friend from Naples to the Faro, or the channel betwixt Naples and Sicily.

" We went always horfe-back : I muft fay for the glory both of our kingdom and government, that we travelled perhaps in the fineft part of Italy, and meet always very bad impracticable roads, very often no inn, or no bed at all, being forced to lye upon the ground : the convents of Capucins, Francifcans, and other religious orders, are the only places where one can be lodged ; but they very feldom have fomething befide ftraw, for to lye upon ; and
then

then buggs, fleas, and all the animals in the world, bite you to nothing.——In many places we could find no convenience for our horfes, or ourfelves; becaufe the generality of the people, they live upon oignons, garlick, and very nafty bread."

In anfwer to Mr. Sharp's account of the beds, the cooks, the poftilions, and the poft-horfes on the Loretto road, Mr. Baretti denies peremptorily, that Mr. Sharp did travel poft, or once entered into a poft-houfe on that road, though Mr. Sharp has fo pofitively afferted it. This inftance might be added to many more, where Mr. Baretti gives Mr. Sharp the flat lye, to the facts he advances ; an argument to which it is difficult to make a fenfible anfwer ; but I who know Mr. Sharp, as I faid before, know that Mr. Baretti has been impofed upon in this cafe, and indeed all the cafes where he has trufted to his informer, as groffly as he himfelf impofes on his readers, when he makes Mr. Sharp expatiate on the extreme wretchednefs of the inhabitants of Ancona ; though Mr. Sharp fpeaks only of the profpect of Ancona, in letter 10, and of the extreme wretchednefs of the peafantry in the neighbourhood of Ancona, in letter 12.

Mr.

Mr. Baretti is however remarkably vehement and diffusive on this groundless charge, and seems to point it out as one of the principal evidences, to prove that Mr. Sharp was difqualified to make obfervations on Italy. He fhould have ftopt a little while, fays he, at Ancona, to have formed a better judgment of that place; neverthelefs, with fubmiffion to Mr. Baretti, I fhould fuppofe, that any body except himfelf will admit, that Mr. Sharp may with propriety fpeak of the profpect of Ancona, without having taken a bed at Ancona.

I fhall not purfue Mr. Baretti in all the attacks he has made on what Mr. Sharp has faid, much lefs on what he has not faid; the detail would be tedious, and very little interefting to the reader. Perhaps I ought to apologize for the following article, relating to Loretto, but I am led to mention it by the uncommon candour of Mr. Baretti on this occafion, who has mifreprefented Mr. Sharp's account but in one particular, I mean that of defcribing the garrifon to confift of 60 or 100 foldiers, which Mr. Sharp fays confifts of 30 only; not but that the increafe of ftrength he has given it, deftroys, in fome degree, the bafis on which Mr. Sharp has grounded his conjecture. Speaking of of the treasures at Loretto, Mr. Sharp has dropt an opinion (not a wish, as Mr. Baretti insinuates) that as the garrison consists only of 30 soldiers, should a Corsair, with a hundred and fifty, or two hundred men, attempt to surprize it, a coup de main well managed, he thinks, might succeed. Mr. Addison too has supposed, that a christian power, who has ships passing to and fro, might without suspicion effect that enterprize.

Instead of considering the hint as good natured, and possibly useful, Mr. Baretti, upon this occasion, rallies with great humour their protestant zeal, and says, if Mr. Addison had examined Loretto, he would not have exposed himself to the ridicule of those Roman catholicks, who know something of the matter. But Mr. Baretti does not seem to attend sufficiently to the rapidity of an action, called a coup de main ; though no man understands the living languages better than himself. What, says he, could such a body of men do, against a garrison of 50 or 60 men, (he will not say more than a hundred) besides the inhabitants in and out of the town ? He asserts too, that the town is tolerably fortified, and the paths to it craggy ; yet I believe the troops that mount-

ed

ed the precipices of Louifbourg and Quebec, would have found a much eafier entrance into Loretto. Neverthelefs to fpeak the truth, the point is merely fpeculative, and hardly worth the time I have beftowed upon it ; though one may be bold to foretell, that fhould an attempt be ever made, the great obftacle to the fuccefs, will not be the number of foldiers and inhabitants, nor the fteepnefs of the hill, nor the tolerablenefs of the fortification, but the difficulty of a Corfair failing up the Adriatick undifcovered, and returning fafely with his plunder to Barbary.

As Mr. Sharp has incurred Mr. Baretti's difpleafure, by infinuating that the poor of Naples chufe the education of a mufical confervatoio, rather than follow a laborious employment, I fhall quote Mr. Baretti on trade, from both his Englifh and Italian opinions.

P. 306. Moft branches of manufactures, fays he in the Englifh account, flourifh amongft the Italians ; and thofe manufactures are purchafed from them by all the commercial world. —Now hear what he fays in his *Frufta Letteraria*, p. 342.—With regard to foreign manufactures, we need only take into our hands, a watch, a cafe, a box, a button, in fhort any

E   bauble

bauble made either in France or in England, to be prefently convinced, that innumerable things manufactured in Italy, ftand in no competition with the fame articles manufactured in thofe countries.

He fays in the 17th chapter of the Englifh account, that however defpicable Mr. Sharp may have reprefented trade, the Italian merchants are looked upon in a very honourable light.—I do not queftion, but that fenfible men there, muft look upon them as promoting the good of their country, which undoubtedly is a very honourable light ; but I believe our gentlemen who have made the tour of Italy, will declare with one voice, that merchants and traders, or the wives of merchants and traders, are feldom or never admitted unmafked to the affemblies of the nobility, either in Florence, Rome, or Naples, and that the nobles are exceedingly punctilious on that article. Indeed, if this were not the fact, how abfurd muft Goldoni's Play of the *Femmine Puntigliofe* (the Punctilious Ladies) have appeared on the Italian theatre ? Wôuid not the audience have immediately hiffed it off the ftage, and declared aloud, that they knew no fuch manners ?—The fable of the play is this : A rich merchant of Leghorn the firft

year

year of his marriage, makes a tour with his wife to Florence; she is exceffively ambitious to be admitted into the converfazioni of quality, which she effects by bribing a certain countefs with a hundred crowns to introduce her; and to fave appearances, she lofes them in the shape of a wager touching the hour of the day, as was previously fettled betwixt them by a mutual confidant. The merchant had quitted trade about three months, which circumftance had flattered his wife that she should find fo much the more eafy accefs; but the whole tenour of the Play proves, that fuch commerce is incompatible. The ladies she is introduced to, upon the difcovery of her rank in life, are extremely affronted, and very rude to her. In the laft fcene, the merchant's wife takes her revenge in expofing the countefs who had received the hundred crowns; and the moral of the Play feems to be fimply this, that we should always feek fuch company who are our equals, and that no one should afpire beyond thofe limits; with which maxim the poet concludes the play.

Mr. Sharp has alfo (in Letter 7th) faid, It is whifpered at Venice, that many of the Nobles are concerned in clandeftine partnerfhips.

Now

Now in fupport of this affertion, and in oppofition to that of Mr. Baretti, who maintains
that the Nobles make no fcruple to appear in
trade, I fhall quote another play of Goldoni,
called *Il Cavalier di buon Gufto*; and as Goldoni is a native, and has been long an inhabitant
of Venice, he may be prefumed to know the
cuftoms of that city. In this comedy the
Count Octavio, who is fuppofed by his extra-
vagance to have wafted his own patrimony,
and the eftate of his nephew, to whom he was
guardian, difcovers in the winding up of the
plot, that he had been enabled to make a
figure in the world, by a clandeftine partner-
fhip with the Venetian merchant Pantaloon;
and takes this opportunity to declare, that commerce does not derogate from the character of a
Cavalier, and it was only in fubmiffion to the
prejudices of the world, that he had chofen to
traffick privately.

We fhall next take a view of what Mr. Baretti and Mr. Sharp have advanced on the fubject of mufick. It was natural for Mr. Sharp,
the moment he arrived at Naples, (the nurfery
both of vocal and inftrumental performers) to
make his firft enquiry upon what footing that
fcience ftood there. He defcribes the magnifi-

cence

cence and vaftnefs of their opera-houfe, the manner of lighting it, the nature of the fub-fcription for the fupport of operas, the falaries of their fingers, &c. &c.

The defcription of the theatre, illuminations, &c. Mr. Baretti affirms to be miferable trifles, and erroneous for the greateft part ; though he grants he was never at Naples, and therefore cannot be fuppofed to be a competent judge of that matter : However, admitting the juftnefs of his animadverfion; yet what regards the cuftoms and manners of Italy on this point, poffibly may not be efteemed frivolous ; and therefore I fhall quote Mr. Baretti himfelf in fupport of the principal facts which Mr. Sharp has alledged.

Mr. Sharp fays, that all the young ladies of fafhion are placed in convents, where mufick is feldom a part of their education : (Mr. Ba-retti has chofen to quote the fift edition, where it is inadvertently afferted to be *no* part of their education ;) wherefore the women of fafhion in Italy are not in general, fo well inftructed in mufick, as the ladies of fafhion in England, Mr. Baretti, who fets out with declaring in his 17th chapter, that he is a ftranger to the tranf-actions of the mufical world, and that he is

equally

equally ignorant of mufick with Mr. Sharp, grants however, that Mr. Sharp was right, when he fays, "Mufick is not much thought of in the education of our young ladies."—Mr. Baretti is pleafed to give us the reafons why Italian ladies are not fo educated: he tells us, that in the warm climate of Italy, the fenfibility of the young ladies is fuch, that (p. 291.) mufick would difcompofe their little hearts; befides, that Italian parents do all they can to guard againft the immoral characters of mufick mafters, as much as Britifh parents in England, do againft the indecencies of the ftage; for, fays he, mufick in Italy gives a voluptuous and wicked turn of mind to the generality of its profeffors and fingers, which laft are defpifed equally with their dancers; befides, he fays, that Italians hold mufick cheap, becaufe they have fo great a plenty of it.

Mr. Sharp has faid, that the opera-houfe is a kind of rendezvous for the polite people, and that they talk loudly during the performance, to the annoyance of thofe who wifh to hear, and to the great mortification of the fingers; and that it is not the cuftom there, as in England, to ufe a wax light, fo that in the pit, it is impoffible for moft men to read the opera,

opera.—A very acute remark, fays Mr. Baretti, (p. 311.) to which I have nothing to fay, but that the Italians are not fo good natured as the Englifh, who have patience enough to run carefully over a ftupid piece of nonfenfe, while a filly eunuch is mincing a vowel into a thoufand invifible particles. When we are at the opera, we confider thofe fellows in the lump, as one of the many things that induced us to be there ; and we pay the fame attention to their finging, which we pay to other parts of that diverfion. We fix our eyes, for in-ftance, a moment or two on the fcenes and the dreffes, when they happen to be new and fuper-latively well imagined ; and our fingers would be very ridiculous indeed, if to their cuftomary impudence they added that of pretending to much more regard than what we pay to the pencil of an ingenious painter, or even to the elegance of a fanciful taylor. And then, though the opera be Metaftafio's, we know for cer-tain beforehand, that it is as perfectly butcher-ed by the Opera Poet, as thofe that are exhi-bited in the Hay-market. This being the cafe, would it not be fupremely ridiculous to pore for fome hours over an opera book with a fmall wax-light in our hands ?—This laft fen-

tence

tence may ferve to juftify Mr. Sharp againft
the reproaches of Mr. Baretti, for his filence
with regard to Metaftafio in his account of
operas and opera-houfes.

Mr. Baretti, in his 29th chapter, fays, that
Mr. Sharp has mifreprefented facts, when he
informs us that the government of Venice re-
ceives private information by the Lyon's mouths,
which are placed in certain parts of the Doge's
palace; for that this method of informing, is
no longer practifed there, and that if Mr. Sharp
had looked into thefe heads, he would have
feen that they have been long full of cobwebs,
and choaked with duft. This latter part of the
affertion, I think I can venture to declare is
not true; and the firft appears queftionable to
me, becaufe it is improbable that fo effential a
change in the conftitution of Venice, fhould
have efcaped the notice of travellers, few of
which omit to mention the Lyon's mouths,
down to the Abbé Richard, and the French
gentleman who publifhed within thefe five
years, his Memoires fur l'Italie par deux gen-
tilfhommes Suedois. The firft of thefe writers
fpeaks of them in vol. 2d. p. 292; the other
in his 2d vol. p. 64.—Befides I know from
Mr. Sharp, that a merchant who refides at
Venice,

Venice, pointed out thefe lyons, and explained their ufe to him. Now that travellers who have made it their bufinefs to examine, and that an inhabitant of Venice, who may be fuppofed to have fome curiofity on this fubject, fhould all agree in efteeming that a notorious truth, which Mr. Baretti reprefents as a notorious falfehood, makes the fact, I fhould imagine, queftionable, and gives fome reafon to fufpect, that Mr. Baretti, by fome accident, has been led into a miftake on this article.

Mr. Sharp has given an opinion in his 15th letter, that certain mufcles in the ftatue of the Farnefian Hercules, are not of the fhape the artift would have given them, had he copied from nature. Mr. Baretti thinks that Glycon was a better judge of the human form than Mr. Sharp, and confequently, that Mr. Sharp's criticifm is prefumptuous. Vol. 2. p. 308.

But though that celebrated ftatuary was a more competent judge of the human form than Mr. Sharp, and might have been a more competent judge alfo of anatomy, had he been furnifhed with the means of cultivating that fcience, yet the fact is, that neither the Greeks nor the Romans were converfant in human diffections,

diffections, nor had their ftatuaries at any time an opportunity of feeing the mufcles of a man artfully denuded. The practice of diffecting brutes only prevailed fo much, even in the time of Galen, that he fpeaks of a human fke-leton at Alexandria, as a fingular phænomenon, and recommends young medical ftudents to go thither from Rome, in order to make them-felves mafters of ofteology.

In the limbs, the flefhy parts of the muf-cles are round and thick, fo that they fwell ex-ceedingly upon inflation, and in athletick men, evidently mark their feveral interflices under the fkin, which is the reafon why Glycon has repre-fented the mufcles of the limbs in their exact fhape and pofition ; but fome of the thin mufcles not fwelling fufficiently in action, to point out their precife boundaries under the fkin, he has probably been obliged, from the want of an original, to fupply with his imagination, a mufculage which is not abfolutely natural. This error is more remarkable in the hinder part of the neck and back, than in any of the other mufcles of the Farnefian Hercules. If you caft an eye on a figure, where the mufcles of the neck and back are diffected, you will obferve the trapezius mufcle poffeffing a large extent of that part.—

part.—Now, were this mufcle as much infla-
ted, as the mufcles of the Farnefian Hercules
are, it would nearly reprefent two triangles
(one on each fide of the fpine) ; but the artift
has not given it that fhape ; wherefore,
with great deference to the amazing genius of
Glycon, we may ftill admit the beauty, but
call in queftion the truth of the mufculage:

I think Mr. Sharp has no where attempted
to give a general character of the Italians.
Probably he knew the difficulty of fuch an attempt, and how liable it would be to cavils,
however well executed. Therefore he has
neither faid that the Italians are learned, or ignorant, witty, or dull, brave, or cowardly,
merciful, or cruel, vindictive, or forgiving,
handfome, or homely ; in fhort, he has mentioned but one character, which he afcribes to
the whole body of the people, from the higheft to the loweft ; I mean the univerfal practice
of fobriety, even to a total exemption from the
vice of drunkennefs.

It is true that Mr. Sharp has taken the freedom to cenfure certain religious ceremonies of
the Italians ; but it does not appear that he
fpoke ludicroufly of them whilft he was in
Italy, and I dare anfwer for him, that he never
once

once in his life uttered a difrefpectful word on
the catholick religion in a catholick country,
or even in the prefence of a catholick in his
own country. He has no where impeached
the principles of their faith, but only thofe
practices, which proteftants efteem fuperftitious mummeries, tending to rob the laity of
their civil rights and privileges ; and though
Mr. Sharp might with great propriety, have
publifhed a defence of proteftantifm' in England, by expofing the follies which ftill fubfift
in Italy, without expecting to be accountable
for it ; yet he was fo unwilling to give offence,
that he apologizes to the catholicks of England,
for this ftep, knowing that many of the wife
and moderate amongft them, wifh they were
well rid of fome of their antient pageantries.
Had Mr. Baretti imitated this conduct, he
would not in the midft of a country, under
whofe laws he enjoys the uncontroled liberty
of faying and writing what he pleafes, have
trefpaffed fo far on that indulgence, as to enter
into a formal vindication of monkery proceffi-
ons, feftivals, &c. and fo indifcreetly brand
the Reformation with the name of the *Great
Sibifm*, (Vide chap. 19. vol. 2.)

But if Mr. Sharp has avoided to give a general

ral character of the Italians, Mr. Baretti has supplied that deficiency in page 374 of his *Frusta Letteraria.*——It is in a letter written by an uncle just returned from his travels, to a beautiful niece. Mr. Baretti says it is worthy of a place in his papers. Here follows an extract from it.

" In this our vile (vigliaca) Italy, it is but too much a shameful custom, when any man sits near a woman, immediately to talk to her in an impudent manner, of unlawful love. Whether she be virgin, wife, or widow, provided she be young, she must be condemned to hear a thousand nauseous whispers from every man who approaches her. It is impossible, my dear Clotilda, but that this must have been often your case, so universally is it the mode in this corrupt country, to insult female modesty."

And in vol. 2d, p. 28. Mr. Baretti tells us, it is proverbially said, that men are every where the same; nevertheless, in my travels through Europe, continues he, I have observed in certain countries, an abundance of individuals of a certain character which are rarely found in other countries. I have not, for example, been able to discover in any other part of Europe,

rope, fuch an infinite number of blockheads (Omaccioni e Omiccatoli) as we fee in Italy, who never diftinguifh good from evil. Would to God that this obfervation were falfe——But alas! it is a truth that our Italy fwarms on every fide, with people, who not only miftake infolence and impudence for vivacity and courage ; impolitenefs and rudenefs for franknefs and fincerity ; naftinefs and beaftlinefs in converfation, for pleafantry and gallantry; but even lies, falfehood, and fometimes treachery itfelf, for acutenefs of parts, ftrength of underftanding, and fuperiority of wifdom, or at leaft for fuperiority of knowledge of the world. I could bring, fays Mr. Baretti, a thoufand and a thoufand proofs of this obfervation, &c. &c.

Mr. Baretti, in his 18th chapter, tells us, that Mr. Sharp and feveral proteftant travellers affert, that the Italians place all their young ladies in convents, and leave them there until they marry, or take the veil ; but that it is a falfhood. Mr. Baretti illuftrates his argument by fuppofing, that in the dutchy of Tufcany there are thirty-fix thoufand young girls, who are able to pay for education ; but that in fact there are fcarcely fix hundred penfioners (board-

ers

ers at convents) in all Tuscany.—By this sup-
position of thirty-six thousand young women,
it appears evidently, that Mr. Baretti and Mr.
Sharp have not turned their thoughts to the
same class of people ; for Mr. Sharp, I believe,
mentions the circumstance of education, only
in two places, the one in letter 19, where he
assigns a reason why the fine ladies at Naples
are not so well instructed in musick as the fine
ladies in London; and in letter 48, where he
accounts for the great number of gentlemen in
comparison of ladies, at the Italian conversa-
zioni. Undoubtedly therefore, Mr. Baretti
has misunderstood Mr. Sharp, who referred
only to the daughters of the nobility and people
of the first families, the numbers of which are
very small, compared with his calculation.

But if the young ladies of fashion are not
educated in convents, it may be asked where
are they educated ? Are not convents in Italy
answerable to our ladies boarding-schools in
England ? However, supposing the majority
of young ladies to be educated elsewhere, that
circumstance would not invalidate the assertion
that few single women are seen at their spectacles, their conversationi, &c. but only the so-
lution of the question, why they are not seen
there ?

there ?—Travellers have afcribed it to the confinement of a convent ; Mr. Baretti has left the
controverfy open, not fpecifying in what manner they are confined. I will neverthelefs
grant to Mr. Baretti, that if it be true that ladies of fafhion are not generally educated in
convents, he has removed one of the moft po-
pular errors under which Englifhmen labour-
ed : But it feems to me, that in arguing this
point he has run himfelf into a difficulty, from
which it will not be eafy to extricate him ; for
if, as he fays, an old maiden is an objeɗ fcarcely ever to be feen in Italy, and if this faɗ is
true alfo of the families of the nobility, it
fhould follow, that as the number of women
is nearly equal to the number of men, and the
number of nuns is but very fmall, it fhould
follow, I fay, that the young men of family
would be all married ; and we ought to fee as
many women in their affemblies (for wives do
not ftay at home) as we fee men ; but the truth
is, that we fee few women in comparifon of
men, which has been hitherto imputed to the
confinement of fingle ladies in their convents.
How Mr. Baretti will clear up this difficulty, I
do not rightly underftand, as it is efteemed an
indifputable faɗ, that few brothers in a noble
family·

family, do marry from a principle of preferving
the family eftate in the name, which by the
cuftom of Italy is divided upon the death of a
father, amongft all the fons.

Page 9. Mr. Baretti likewife afferts, that Italians in general are very forry when their girls
take it into their filly heads to become nuns;
and fo far are they from clapping them forcibly,
or even chearfully into a nunnery, that they
do all in their power to reconcile them to the
world ; fometimes they ridicule them, fometimes they fcold them, and fometimes they
carry them to mafquerades, operas, and publick walks, where young men ogle, bow, and
whifper, &c.

This may poffibly be a true reprefentation
of the manners of Italy in regard to nunneries,
and the education of young ladies of fafhion ;
but it may likewife be doubted ; for though a
foreigner cannot guard too much againft mif-
taking fingularities for cuftoms, yet I muft
mention one inftance under my own obfervation, which clafhes with the doctrine laid down
by Mr. Baretti.——When I was at Naples I had
the honour of a card from a noble duke, whofe
daughter was to take the veil, inviting me to
attend at the ceremony of her profeffion. This

F   duke

duke had many daughters, fome of whom had already taken the veil, and fo little forrow did I perceive (upon the lofs of another daughter) either in his countenance, or the countenance of his friends, that the chearfulnefs of their behaviour and vivacity of their converfation after the function, was the circumftance which ftruck me moft particularly in the occurrences of that day.

Mr. Baretti, chap. 6. p. 4. ridicules the opinion that in Italy matches are generally the effects of parental authority, and not of mutual affections amongft the young people who fometimes, according to Mr. Sharp, do not fee each other more than once or twice before the celebration of their marriage; neverthelefs though it may be difficult to prove in a diftant country, what is a matter of notoriety in another country, I fhall hazard from Goldoni, a kind of proof that in Italy it is a common cuftom among the gentry, I mean to difpofe of children in marriage without their participation. Goldoni fays, that his Serva Amorofa (the Amorous Waiting-maid) was one of his moft fortunate productions, and met with the greateft fuccefs. I fhall therefore fuppofe, that the favourite character in it, Corallina, could hard-

ly

ly have given us a picture of their manners, ut-
terly repugnant to truth ; yet in one scene of
the comedy, she expresses herself in the following words. "It would be extremely right
says she, if in this business of matrimony, the
young couple might speak once at least to each
other without coutroul, and to be secure of a
reciprocal affection before they were contracted."
But without Goldoni's assistance, I might have
brought an undeniable authority from Mr. B.
himself, who in page 95 alledges, that the
Great generally marry for the sake of alliance or
interest, without much consulting inclination.

I am now come to the article of Cicisbeism.
The account Mr. Sharp has given of its
present state in Venice, Florence, Naples,
and Rome, has drawn upon him the heaviest
imputations from Mr. Baretti ; but I shall not
enter into the examination of this part of Mr.
Sharp's letters, before I give the substance of
what he has advanced on this head.—He says
that in Venice, a gentleman who attends on,
or gallants a married lady, is called a Cavaliere
servente, and in the other parts of Italy a Cicisbeo. This Cicisbeo waits on her to the
Spectacles, the Converfazioni, and Corso (the
publick

publick walks): He says, that hufbands do not
appear at thefe places in the company of their
wives; nor will fashion allow one woman to
conduct another, fo that they become con-
strained to admit of Cicifbeo's, unlefs they will
condefcend to live always at home, which cannot be expected from women of diftinction,
who alone affume the privilege of appearing
with their Cicifbeos, and of whom alone Mr.
Sharp muft neceffarily fpeak. He goes on to
tell us, that the character of Cicifbeo is not un-
derftood to be an innocent one; and that the
ladies are fuppofed not to live in greater purity
with them than with their hufbands, and generally fpeaking, with much lefs. That the
hufbands have their revenge in being the Cicifbeos to other ladies; that the prefent ftate of
Cicifbeifm in Italy is a greater revolution in the
manners of a people, than probably can be in-
ftanced in any other country; for that formerly
hufbands were jealous, and immured their
wives, but that now Italian ladies have more
liberty than any other women in Europe:
That notwithftanding the notoriety of the
practice, all the ladies behaved with fo much
modefty and decorum, that he was almoft
tempted to treat the reports he had heard as
mere

mere detraction. That spending so many evenings at the envoy's palace in Naples, where the foreign ministers and the first quality of Naples resorted, he had the opportunity of seeing there great numbers of ladies, with their Cicisbeo's, who visited and associated together in the same manner that plain men do with their wives in England. I believe I have here given the most essential part of the description.

It must be granted that the account seems strange and incredible; and a man who should contradict Mr. Sharp would easily find credit from every one who has not been in Italy, and from every one who has not lived in Italy, amongst people of the first rank there; for I do not question but that there are many natives of that country who are ignorant of what passes in the great world.

But Mr. Baretti says that it is impossible to be true; that could the Italians read so much illiberal abuse, and ferocious declamation on them and their manners, they would stare, and many of the ladies would certainly wish him for a while under the tuition of some good exorcist; and that he never will be able to persuade the world there is a vast tract of land in a christian country, where some hundred thou-

sands

fands of hufbands are moft regularly and moft infamoufly wronged by their wives, &c.

Mr. Baretti in this place, as in many others, in order to involve Mr. Sharp in abfurdity, fhifts the propofition from particulars to generals, from the narrow circle of the polite world, who only have adopted this fpecies of gallantry, to all ranks and claffes of people, to fome hundreds of thoufands, fays Mr. Baretti. I prefume however, that Mr. Baretti will not deny that few young married ladies of diftinction (I might fay old married ladies) are feen without their cicifbeos ; that hufbands do not appear in publick with their wives, but that their wives are accompanied by the cicifbeos ; that look into a coach at the Corfo, the gentleman and lady you fee in it are not a hufband and wife, but a wife and cicifbeo ; that cicifbeo's have the opportunity of many private converfations with their ladies both at home and abroad, from the hour of rifing to the hour of going to bed.—— But, fays Mr. Baretti, granting all this to be true, the commerce betwixt cicifbeos and their ladies, except in a few inftances, is ftill innocent, which innocence of behaviour he afcribes to a fpirit of chivalry derived from their anceftors, and to Platonick notions which prevail all
over

over Italy. Almost all the polite Italians, says he, imbibe such sentiments as soon as they acquire the power of reading, and learn that the contemplation of earthly beauty raises an honest mind to the contemplation and love of the heavenly (p. 104.); in short, according to Mr. Baretti, to cicisbee a lady, means only to whisper a lady, the old word cicisbeare bearing that import: but, adds he, Mr. Sharp knows nothing of the matter, through an ignorance of our language and poetry, particularly the writings of Petrarch, which would have served as a key to our general customs and manners.

It is however a little extraordinary that he should suppose this private intercourse betwixt ladies and their cicisbeos to be so very pure, when he admits that the young ladies have such a sensibility peculiar to the climate of Italy, that they are not to be trusted at their harpsichords with the languishings of a *Mi sento morir*, set to musick by a feeling composer, nor with the company of musick-masters, for a great inconvenience; what the inconvenience is Mr. Baretti leaves us to imagine (p. 299.); but in England, says he, where the temperature of the climate is a guard against these lively impressions, young ladies may safely apply to musick.

I shall

I shall not oppose Mr. Baretti on the nature of our climate ; but notwithstanding this phlegm which he ascribes to the constitution of our English young ladies, I can assure him that were any of our married women to dedicate their private hours to a certain individual, were they to appear at his elbow in all places of resort, at routs, drums, &c. tho' they lay every night in their husband's bed, their phlegm would not exempt them from the suspicion of intrigue, which would be esteemed, even in this climate, un-avoidable in the midst of so many opportuni-ties ; and such ladies would certainly be stigma-tized and shunned.

. These reasonings I may be told are plausible, but not convincing, and that better and more positive proofs are necessary to persuade an English reader that these manners are not the fancy of Mr. Sharp's brains, but the real man-ners of the great cities in Italy. To produce a proof from the writings of respectable Italian authors, that he has said nothing but what has been said by them before, might have probably been a difficult task. Should an Italian, after his return from England, assert that in some of the great streets in London, multitudes of pro-stitutes walk there for the purpose of seduction,

without

without giving umbrage either to magiſtracy or the neighbourhood, he might be charged with falſhood, and called upon for his proofs, which however he might not be furniſhed with, though the fact be ſo notorious :—this fortunately is not my caſe ; I have in my hands certain writings which throw ſome light on this controverſy, and I believe eſtabliſh the truth of what Mr. Sharp has advanced.

Mr. Baretti ſays (p. 204.) that foreigners ſhould look for ſure information concerning our cuſtoms and manners in the poem of Paſſeroni of Milan, and not in the idle and ſhallow performances of Mr. Sharp and other ſuch conceited and ignorant travellers. At Milan, he ſays, there is likewiſe one Parini, who will certainly prove a very eminent poet, if he continues to write. His *Mattino* and *Mezzodi* have filled me with hopes that he will ſoon be the Pope, or the Boileau of Italy, as he is already almoſt equal to them in juſtneſs of thinking, and exactneſs of expreſſion, and ſeems to ſurpaſs them in richneſs of imagery and fecundity of invention.

As Parini is celebrated for his juſtneſs of thinking, and exactneſs of expreſſion, I ſhall lay before the reader what he thinks and ſays

on

on cicifbeifm, in his poem called *Il Mattino*
(the Morning).—This poem is defigned to expofe the reigning vices and follies of the prefent
age in Italy ; and is therefore dedicated to
Fafhion. It is a picture of a luxurious young
man of high birth, fitting up all night, and ly-
ing in bed all the morning, with his fidlers, his
taylors, his dancing-mafters, &c. attending at
his levee. When the poet has defcribed his
valet de chambres, his frifeurs, &c. adorning
his perfon, he addreffes himfelf to the hero of
his piece, and fays, It is now time you fhould
confider of the companion whom heaven has
deftined for you, to divide the burthen of an
idle life——Do you grow pale ? I do not fpeak
of marriage ; I fhould be a mufty fellow indeed to give fuch foolifh antiquated counfel.—
Then rallying the ftate of matrimony, he fays,
" May he perifh who advifes you to marriage."
Neverthelefs you fhall have a partner, who is
young, and who is the wife of another, fince
the inviolable cuftom of the polite world, of
which you are a member, will have it fo.

Pera dunque chi a te nozze configlia,
Ma nonperò fenza compagna andrai,
Che fia Giovane Dama, ed al trui Spofa ;
Poichè

Poichè sì vuole in violabil rito
Del bel mondo, onde tu fè cittadino——

Afterwards the poet enters into a detail of this revolution in the manners of Italy, which he illuftrates by the following allegory ; of which I fhall give an imperfect tranflation.

In antient times the mother of Cupid placed him under the care of his brother Hymen, becaufe fhe was afraid that being blind he might wander and lofe his way, and alfo that he would not be able to direct his arrows fo as to preferve the human race ; therefore fhe gave orders that he fhould fhoot the arrows and Hymen fhould direct them. Thus the fweet couple went always in thofe days, hand in hand, every fhepherd and fhepherdefs were united in the bands of wedlock. Sol faw them together all the day, fitting by the fountain, or the purling ftream ; and Diana beheld them all the night in the happy nuptial bed, which the two Gods ftrewed moft plentifully with lilies and with rofes. But when the wings of Cupid had acquired fufficient ftrength, he mounted the fkies, and with a furious countenance, entering Olympus, and brandifhing his bow of fteel, he loudly proclaimed, I will fway

the

the fcepter alone—Then turning to his mother, he faid, Shall Cupid, the moft powerful amongft the Gods, and the firft-born of Venus, receive law from a vile younger brother ? Shall I not dare to ftrike the fame heart more than once, becaufe it fo pleafes that dirty fellow ? Shall I never have it in my power, after I have faften-ed a knot, to loofe it, aye, and faften it again if it be my pleafure ? Shall I fuffer him to daub my arrows with his unguents, and weaken their poifon, that they may more fafely enter the human breaft ? Why does he not alfo rob me of my bow and quiver, and leave me naked, a mere outcaft of the Gods ?— O the charming life were he to reign in my place ! What a fcene of ridiculoufnefs to view him throwing about ice inftead of fire, and impotently ex-erting himfelf to drive wearinefs and averfion from languid fouls ! Therefore, dear mother, hearken ; I find that I am able, and I will reign alone : Divide the power betwixt us in the manner which may be moft agreeable to you, but fo that mankind for the future may not find me in the company of Hymen.—The Citherean Goddefs endeavoured to footh his paffion ; fhe begged, fhe wept, but all in vain : wherefore, addreffing herfelf to her two funs,

9   fhe

she compofed the quarrel in the following words : Since then there can be no peace betwixt you, let your government be divided; and that one brother may be always feparated from the other, let your hours and your occupations be different. You who are fo impetuous and fo proud of your darts, be it your province to wound the foul and govern by day; and you, who are crowned with rofes, let it be your charge to couple *mere bodies*, and with your flaming torch take the command by night. Hence, continues he, is derived that polite mode, which grants to hufbands the dark hours, and the chafte bodies of their wives; and to you, O moft bleffed and moft noble race of men, the hearts of thofe very wives, and an abfolute command by day.

Should Mr. Baretti urge that this is a poem, and that great allowances are to be made for the exaggerations of poetry, I fhall only obferve, that Parini, who is fo *juft in his thinking*, and fo *exact in his expreffion*, has defcribed the prefent ftate of cicifbeifm (were the poem ftript of its poetical ornaments) juft as Mr. Sharp has defcribed it, and I prefume juft as it now ftands :—but if poetry be infufficient, I hope what Mr. Baretti himfelf has given us in profe

profe on this fubject will prove more fatisfactory. It is in his *Frufta Letteraria*, Vol. 1. p.
184, where he has written an imaginary
letter from a bride to her hufband, and fays,
fuch kind of letters would be more ufeful to
the world, than the epithalamiums, &c. now
in vogue upon every marriage. Here follows
an extract from it.

" Though I am young, I know the wicked-
nefs of the age, I know that feveral men will
be, or pretend to be, enamoured of me, as
foon as the hurry of my wedding, and a few
of my bridal days are over. I know that more
than one of your deareft friends will not let
flip the opportunity of dropping privately fweet
and flattering infinuations, to induce me to
break my matrimonial vow; and I know that
few, very few, will fcruple to rob you of the
heart of your wife; and to contaminate and
corrupt it. One will attack me with humble
language, another with down-caft looks, another
with prefents, another with procuring me diver-
fions, another with free converfation, another
with obfcenity, and another with different un-
juft methods; but I will ftand firmly like a
tower of brafs, &c.—Neverthelefs, dear hufband, it will be neceffary on the other hand,
that in fpite of *irrefiftable Fafhion*, you fhall

I

never be afhamed of being feen with me, *even in publick* ; that you fhall not blufh to confefs you love me ; however fuch a confeffion may fometimes expofe a married man to the derifion of fools. It will be neceffary that you not only refrain from acting as a Cicifbeo, or Cavaliere Servente, though with an intention to pafs your time innocently ; but you muft alfo take care to keep me in the opinion, even after the firft month of our marriage, that you prefer me to every other creature of my fpecies."

To the inftances which have already been given of the manner in which Mr. Sharp's Letters have been quoted by Mr. Baretti, the following are added, that the reader may be better able to judge of the criticifms which he has founded on fuch quotations.

Mr. Sharp, in his 19th Letter, fays, That mufical talents are rewarded in England tenfold above what they are in Naples, *except* in the fingle inftance of the firft clafs of Opera Singers, who are paid extravagantly. To give this obfervation the appearance of abfurdity, Mr. Baretti, Vol. 1. p. 148. quotes Mr. Sharp as faying in one line that the Opera performers are not paid fo liberally as in London ; and in the next, that Gabrieli had for one year only, nine hundred Englifh pounds. Mr.

Mr. Sharp, in Letter 51, fays, That he faw people making hay in the fmall plots of the King of Sardinia's gardens at Turin. Mr. Baretti, Vol. 2. p. 216. makes him fay that the King of Sardinia *fells grafs.*

Mr. Baretti, in Vol. 2. p. 76. charges Mr. Sharp with having refided two months in a town, where the Friars are more numerous than in any other in Europe, and having nothing more to fay of them but that they are fuperftitious, and have *fat guts*; but the words *fat guts* are not to be found in Mr. Sharp's Letters.

To give a ridiculous turn to Mr. Sharp's defcription of the Opera Houfe at Naples, Mr. Baretti tells us, that he *meafured with his eye the amazing extent*, &c. Vol. 1. p. 169. Mr. Baretti has here, in his cuftomary manner, ufed Italics, intimating that they are the very words of Mr. Sharp, which is not the fact.

Mr Sharp in Letter 10th, alluding to the triumphant ftate of the Church in the Ecclefiaftical dominions, fays, That *every place labours here* under great difadvantages; from the infinite conceffions that are made to the Church, by the commercial and military parts of the nation. Mr. Baretti, to render him ridiculous, changes the words *every place labours*

labours here, for the words *Ancona lies here*, &c. by which contrivance he makes Mr. Sharp fay that of the fmall town of Ancona, which is really faid of the whole nation; and then proceeds very gayly to inform us, that he never heard at Ancona of the Anconitan nation. Vol. 1ft, p. 13.

Vol. 2d, p. 315. Mr. Baretti makes Mr. Sharp affirm, that whether you travel with Voiturins, or by the Poft, through Savoy, you ftill advance at the fame flow rate. The whole of this extract is a fiction; for neither the opinion, nor one word of the fentence is to be found in Sharp's Letters. Mr. Sharp has faid no more than what is contained in the following paragraph.—A man may travel poft, if he pleafes, through the Alps; but it is attended with fome trouble; and as I would not advife any one to drive faft on the edges of thofe precipices, I fhall forbear to enter into any detail on that fubject. Vide the admonition, annexed to the Letters.

I prefume the reader is now perfuaded that the greater part of the heavy cenfures drawn down upon Mr. Sharp are either for words which he never faid, or for words which Mr. Baretti himfelf had nearly faid before him.

G   What

What may have led Mr. Baretti into this over-
fight I cannot pofitively determine, but he has
told us, that were Italians indulged with the
liberty of the prefs, they would certainly
make an illiberal ufe of it ; and perhaps a fond-
nefs to fupport, at all events, that cruel charge
againft his countrymen, may have prompted
him to give the world a pregnant example of
the truth of it in his own writings.

F · I N I S.